MERCER MAYER'S LC + THE CRITTER KIDS®

BACKSTAGE PASS

A Golden Book • New York

Western Publishing Company, Inc., Racine, Wisconsin 53404

A Mercer Mayer Ltd./J. R. Sansevere Book

Copyright © 1995 Mercer Mayer Ltd. All rights reserved.
Printed in the U.S.A. No part of this book may be reproduced or copied
in any form without written permission from the publisher.
Critter Kids® is a Registered Trademark of Mercer Mayer.
School Time™ is a trademark of Mercer Mayer Ltd.
All other trademarks are the property of Western Publishing Company, Inc.
Library of Congress Catalog Card Number: 94-79456
ISBN: 0-307-16031-9/ISBN: 0-307-66031-1 (lib. bdg.)   A MCMXCV

Written by Erica Farber/J. R. Sansevere

LC

VELVET

LITTLE SISTER

TIGER

KOOL BEAR

SLICK RICK

SU SU   GABBY   TIMOTHY

GATOR   FLEX   HENRIETTA

LC and his two best friends, Tiger and Gator, were in their clubhouse. They were listening to music and playing a game they had made up called "Guess the Rock Star."

It was LC's turn. He jumped up on the table. He bent his knees and played air guitar with one hand. With his other hand, he made a peace sign over his head. "Guess who I am?" LC yelled.

"Spaz!" said Tiger.

"The lead singer of Critter Jam," said Gator.

They slapped each other five.

"Yep," said LC. "Spaz is the coolest dude!"

Tiger and Gator both nodded.

"One day I want to be a rock star just like Spaz!" said LC.

Just then Little Sister barged into the clubhouse. "Time for dinner!" Little Sister yelled.

LC jumped, tripped on his untied shoelace, and fell right off the table onto the floor.

"What were you doing on the table anyway?" Little Sister asked.

"The dude was jamming," said Tiger.

"Yeah, he was Spaz from Critter Jam," explained Gator.

"Spaz is yucky," said Little Sister. "He has fake hair."

"No, he doesn't," said LC. "Spaz is the most awesome rock star in the world. And one day I'm gonna be a rock star just like him."

"You can't be a rock star," said Little Sister. "You don't even have a guitar."

LC sighed. Little Sister was right. Every rock star needed a guitar.

The Critters all sat down to dinner.

"Guess what LC wants to be when he grows up?" asked Little Sister.

"What?" said Mr. Critter.

"A rock star," said Little Sister. "And he doesn't even know how to play the guitar."

"That's because I don't have one," said LC.

"If I had a guitar I could learn how to play."

"Well, I happen to have a banjo you could use," said Mr. Critter. "You know, I was quite a banjo player in my day."

"A banjo's not the same as a guitar," said LC.

"Well, it's a good way to learn the basics," said Mr. Critter. "I'll look for it after dinner."

After dinner LC and Little Sister went to watch TV in the living room.

"Hey, Little Sister, let's watch CTV," said LC.

"No way!" said Little Sister.

LC grabbed the remote control. He clicked on CTV just as *KAYNE'S WORLD* came on. "I have an important announcement to make," said Kayne.

"I'm gonna miss *Critter Hills, 12345*," yelled Little Sister.

"Shhh!" said LC. "I've got to hear this."

"We're live here at CTV," said Kayne. "Welcome to *KAYNE'S WORLD*. Tonight we have a special guest, Spaz, the lead singer of the world's most happening band—Critter Jam!"

"Wow!" said LC. "Spaz!"

"Tonight Spaz has something big to tell all of you Critter Jam fans," said Kayne.

"Critter Jam is coming to Critterville," said Spaz.

"And the first one hundred critters to buy tickets," said Kayne, "get free backstage passes. Tickets go on sale Saturday at ten o'clock. And they're only ten dollars. Be there or be square!"

Little Sister grabbed the remote control and switched the channel to her show.

"Ooooh," said Little Sister to the TV. "I knew he was gonna ask her to the prom."

Just then Mr. Critter walked into the living room. He was playing his banjo.

"Dad, I'm watching a show!" yelled Little Sister.

"I'm sorry, Little Sister," said Mr. Critter. "Well, here's the banjo, son," he said.

LC just stared at the banjo. What good was a banjo, he thought. He had to get one of those backstage passes. He just had to . . .

The next morning when LC got to school, he
went to his locker to unpack his books.

"Hey, dude, did you see *KAYNE'S WORLD* last
night?" asked Tiger.

"Yep," said LC.

"We've got to get tickets," said Timothy.

"Yeah," said LC. "And we've got to make sure
we get there early enough to get those backstage
passes."

"I've got my ten dollars," said Gator.

"Me too," said Tiger. "Good thing it wasn't any
more than that or I wouldn't have enough."

16

The boys ran over to Su Su's locker.

"Where's the bug?" asked Tiger.

"There is no bug," said Su Su. "My daddy got me front-row tickets to the Critter Jam concert and Gabby, Velvet, Henrietta, and I are all going!"

"So eat your hearts out," said Gabby.

"Oh, yeah," said LC. "Well, we're getting back-stage passes. We're gonna meet Spaz himself."

"Yeah," said Tiger. "And play his guitar."

"Right," said Su Su. "Let's see your passes."

"We don't have them yet," said LC. "We're getting them tomorrow when we buy our tickets."

"You mean you think you're going to be one of the first one hundred critters on line," said Gabby. "Good luck!"

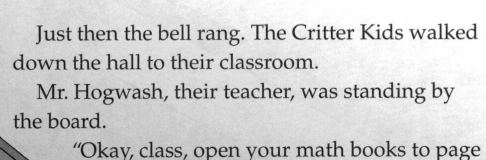

Just then the bell rang. The Critter Kids walked down the hall to their classroom.

Mr. Hogwash, their teacher, was standing by the board.

"Okay, class, open your math books to page 54," said Mr. Hogwash. "Gabby, would you please read the problem out loud to the class?"

Gabby cleared her throat.

"Mr. Green had ten dollars," Gabby read. "First he bought a beautiful scarf for Mrs. Green that cost four dollars. Then he bought candy for himself that cost three dollars and fifty cents. How much money did Mr. Green have left?"

LC started to work out the problem. First he subtracted four dollars from the ten. Suddenly LC remembered that he had spent four of his ten dollars on comics. Next he subtracted the three dollars and fifty cents Mr. Green had spent on candy. Oh, no, LC thought to himself, he had spent that much on candy, too.

"How much money does Mr. Green have left?" asked Mr. Hogwash.

"Two fifty!" shouted LC. "It's not enough for a Critter Jam ticket! They're ten dollars."

Everyone laughed.

"You're right, Mr. Critter," said Mr. Hogwash. "Lucky for Mr. Green he's not going to the Critter Jam concert."

LC sighed. It looked like he wasn't going to the Critter Jam concert either unless he could come up with exactly seven dollars and fifty cents by tomorrow.

When school was over, LC and the boys walked slowly home.

"What are you going to do now?" asked Gator.

"Yeah, dude," said Tiger. "How are you going to get the rest of the money so you can go to the Critter Jam concert?"

LC didn't answer. He didn't know what to say.

"Why don't you ask your mom and dad for the money?" asked Timothy.

"Because they'll say I've got to earn it," said LC.

"That's it!" said Tiger. "We'll help you earn it."

"All you've got to do is get your mom and dad to give you a bunch of chores," said Gator. "And we'll do them first thing in the morning before we go get the tickets."

"That's a great idea!" said LC. "Let's go to my house right now and see what chores my mom has for us to do."

The boys ran all the way to LC's house.

"Hi, Mom," said LC. "You look pretty today."

"You sure do, Mrs. Critter," said Tiger. Timothy and Gator both nodded.

"Look out, Mom," said Little Sister. "They're up to something."

"No, we're not," said LC. "It's just that we wanna go to this concert and I was gonna pay for my ticket with the ten dollars Grandma gave me, but I forgot that I spent some of it."

"How much?" asked Little Sister.

"Just seven dollars and fifty cents," said LC.

"Why, that means you already spent most of your money," said Mrs. Critter. "I can't just give you that much money."

"I don't want you to give me the money, Mom," said LC. "I just want you to give me some chores so that I can earn it."

"I'm sorry, LC," said Mrs. Critter. "But I don't have any chores for you to do right now."

The boys went outside to play football. Tiger threw the ball to LC.

LC caught it. "Now what?" he asked.

"I did all the chores at my house," said Tiger.

"Me too," said Gator.

Just then Mrs. Crabtree walked out onto her porch and down her front steps. She put up a sign in her yard. It said YARD WORK $12.

"That's it!" Tiger shouted, pointing to the sign.

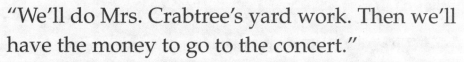

"We'll do Mrs. Crabtree's yard work. Then we'll have the money to go to the concert."

"Do you know how to do yard work?" asked Timothy.

"Sure," said LC, "I've watched my mom mow our lawn many times. It's a piece of cake."

"And weeding's real easy, too," said Tiger.

"I bet Mrs. Crabtree is picky," said Gator.

"Don't worry about it," said Tiger. "Let's go."

LC and the boys ran over to Mrs. Crabtree's house. They walked up the steps to her front porch. LC took a deep breath and rang the bell. Nothing happened.

"Ring it again," said Tiger.

LC rang the bell again.

"Hold your horses," called a grumpy voice. "I'll be right there."

Finally Mrs. Crabtree opened the door. "I don't want any," she said.

"We're . . . uh . . . here about the sign," said LC.
"We can do your yard work," said Tiger.
"Hmmm, I don't know," said Mrs. Crabtree.
"We'll do it for less than twelve dollars," said
LC. "We'll do it for ten dollars."
"Well, in that case, okay," said Mrs. Crabtree.
"But you boys better know what you're doing."

Early the next morning the boys met at
Mrs. Crabtree's house.

"How do we know what are weeds and what
are flowers?" asked Gator.

"Just pull up all the green stuff," said Tiger.

"Yeah," said LC. "The more you pull the better."

"Are you sure?" asked Gator.

"Sure I'm sure," said LC.

All four boys began to pull out Mrs. Crabtree's
weeds, flowers, and plants. They weeded until
they made a huge pile.

Then LC went to get the lawnmower.

"Can one of you guys help me?" asked LC. "This mower is really heavy."

Timothy, Tiger, and Gator made a running leap and threw their bodies against the mower.

Suddenly the mower began to roll down the hill. The boys tried to stop it, but it was too late. The mower rolled faster and faster. It was heading straight for Mrs. Crabtree's fence!

Suddenly there was a loud bang. Mrs. Crabtree bolted out of bed and ran over to her window.

"Aaahhh!" Mrs. Crabtree screamed. She ran downstairs and outside. "You wrecked my yard!" she yelled. "I'm not paying you anything!"

LC and the boys looked down at the ground.

"In fact, you owe me exactly thirty-two dollars and fifty cents for the mess," said Mrs. Crabtree.

The boys didn't say a word. They knew Mrs. Crabtree was right.

They took out all their money. It came to exactly thirty-two dollars and fifty cents. They handed it to Mrs. Crabtree. Now no one could go to the Critter Jam concert.

The boys walked slowly out of Mrs. Crabtree's yard and sat down on the curb. Just then the girls came walking down the street.

"You guys are a mess," said Su Su.

"Hey, weren't you supposed to get your tickets for the Critter Jam concert today?" asked Gabby.

"Yeah," said Henrietta. "What about your backstage passes?"

"We're working on it," said LC.

"I heard on the radio that all the tickets sold out already," said Velvet.

"I knew all along you guys weren't going to get backstage passes," said Su Su.

"Well, we've got to go," said Gabby.

"Where are you going?" Timothy asked.

"We're going to see Spaz," said Su Su. "He's staying at the Critter Hotel."

"Yeah," said Gabby. "Anybody who's anyone will be there."

"See ya later," said Velvet.

"I've got a great idea!" said LC. "Let's go down to the Critter Hotel and meet Spaz, too."

"I'm sure he'll have extra tickets to the concert," said Tiger.

"Cool!" said Gator.

The boys took off down the block. When they got to the Critter Hotel, they ran up the front steps. They all squished into one of the revolving doors. They flew through the door and landed in a heap on the lobby floor.

The manager stared at the boys' messy clothes and frowned. He rang a bell on his desk.

Suddenly a big security guard grabbed the boys by their collars.

"No dirty kids allowed at the Critter Hotel," said the guard.

Before the boys could say a word, the guard threw them out of the back door of the hotel.

At that moment a limo pulled up to the back entrance of the hotel. A guy in a black suit climbed out. He looked over at the boys.

"Hey, you!" he said. "I'm Critter Jam's manager. And I want you to take this stuff upstairs."

"Who, us?" said LC.

"Yeah, you," said the manager.

Suddenly Spaz got out of the limo.

"Wow!" said the boys. They jumped up and ran toward the limo. They began to pick up the bags.

"Be careful with that one," said Spaz, pointing to an instrument case. "That's my baby."

"Okay," said LC. He turned to Tiger. "It must be his guitar," LC whispered. He picked up the case very carefully. Then he and the boys followed Spaz and his manager back into the hotel.

They all took the elevator up to Critter Jam's suite. When they opened the door, they saw four teenagers having a snack.

"Hey, who are you guys?" asked the manager.

"We're your roadies," said the tallest teenager.

"Our roadies?!" said the manager.

"If you're our roadies, then who are these guys?" Spaz asked, pointing to LC and the boys.

"Beats me," said the smallest teenager.

"Well, you guys are fired for not being down-stairs on time," said the manager.

"And you dudes will be our roadies for the concert tonight," said Spaz.

"Cool!" yelled LC, Tiger, Gator, and Timothy.

It was almost time for the Critter Jam concert to begin. Su Su, Gabby, Velvet, and Henrietta stood in the crowd. They were so far back that they could hardly see the stage.

"Some front-row seats your dad got," said Henrietta. "I'm glad I brought my binoculars."

"Well, at least we're here," said Su Su.

"The boys didn't even get to come," said Gabby.

"And they thought they were going to get passes to go backstage," said Velvet.

Suddenly the stage lights went on. The crowd began to cheer.

"Oh, my gosh!" Henrietta yelled.

"What?" said Gabby. She grabbed the binoculars out of Henrietta's hands. "No way!"

"Let me see," said Su Su. She snatched the binoculars from Gabby. "It can't be!" she yelled.

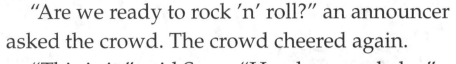

"Are we ready to rock 'n' roll?" an announcer
asked the crowd. The crowd cheered again.
"This is it," said Spaz. "Hand me my baby."
LC picked up the instrument case and brought
it over to Spaz. He was sure that inside it
must be the coolest guitar ever.

LC watched Spaz open the case. He couldn't believe his eyes. Spaz's baby wasn't a guitar—it was a banjo, just like his dad's!

"Your baby is a banjo?!" LC said.

"Yeah, dude," said Spaz. "I always start off every concert with my banjo. My dad gave it to me when I was just about your age. Ever since then I knew I was gonna be a rock star."

"Wow!" said LC.

"Now let's rock 'n' roll!" yelled Spaz.

It was the greatest concert LC and the Critter Kids had ever seen. When LC got home, he had only one thing on his mind.

"Dad," said LC. "Where's your banjo?"

"It's right here," said Mr. Critter.

LC picked up the banjo. "You're never going to believe this," LC said. "But the greatest rock star in the world played a banjo before he ever played a guitar."

Mr. Critter smiled as LC strummed the banjo.